透明な迷宮

平野啓一郎

UEA PUBLISHING PROJECT
NORWICH

The Transparent Labyrinth

Keiichirō Hirano

Translated
by
Kerim Yasar

The Transparent Labyrinth
Keiichirō Hirano

Translated from the Japanese by
Kerim Yasar

First published by
Strangers Press, Norwich, 2017
part of UEA Publishing Project

Distributed by
NBN International

Printed by
Swallowtail Print, Norwich

All rights reserved
© Keiichirō Hirano, 2017
Translation © Kerim Yasar, 2014

Series editors
David Karashima
Elmer Luke

Editorial team
Kate Griffin
Nathan Hamilton
Philip Langeskov

Cover design and typesetting
Nigel Aono–Billson
Glen Robinson

Illustration and Design © Nigel Aono-Billson, 2017

ISBN-13: 978-1911343080

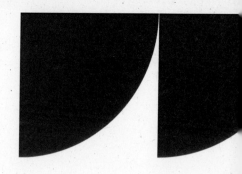

LONG BEFORE femme fatales dominated the silver screen, they came to life in the pages of Jun'ichirō Tanizaki's fiction. In his first major story, written in 1910, 'The Tattooer', a man sedates a beautiful young woman and inscribes a giant spider across her back. What seems like an act of violation turns on its head, as the woman begins to exercise an erotic power over Tanizaki's hero far greater than his ink gun possessed over her skin. In the end it is he who is tattooed, not her.

Reading Tanizaki today, it's hard to believe some of his work is over 100 years old. Written in the Meiji Era, as old ways collapsed and the influence of the West pushed in, Tanizaki's fiction twists around unleashed forces of desire and humiliation. The novels are full of dangerous dames whose power over men comes from their unattainability, their withholding, their unknowability. In his early period, Tanizaki experienced this power dynamic intimately. Tanizaki had encouraged his unhappy wife to engage in an affair with a writer friend – hoping it'd alleviate her melancholy.

Later in his life, Tanizaki would leave Tokyo and reorient himself toward more traditional aspects of Japanese culture. Until then, though, two novelists in particular held an outsized influence over Tanizaki: Edgar Allan Poe and Oscar Wilde, the twinned creators of horror and the grotesque. One feels the imprint of their influence on the story you hold in your hand, 'The Transparent Labyrinth', by Keiichirō Hirano. Born in 1975,

Hirano is such a modern writer that he feels 100 years old, too.

The story is compellingly simple. A Japanese businessman travels to Hungary to meet with clients. After his appointment, he meanders about a city and gets lost. He sits down at a café to recover his bearings and immediately loses them further when he meets eyes with a Japanese woman named Misa. They begin to speak in Japanese and her story ought to have set off all kinds of warning lights in Hirano's narrator's mind. Instead it compels him more.

Misa has been traveling around Europe for months and is now in a kind of debt to an Italian woman, who sits beside Misa possessively, eyeing Hirano's narrator suspiciously. Sensing a woman at risk, Hirano's narrator unwisely joins their table and then follows them to a party across town. At the soirée something terrible and strange happens which will mark Hirano's narrator for the rest of his life. It is not clear whether it is a game, or a form of torture. The result of the incident means that Hirano's narrator cannot simply disengage from Misa. He feels bound to her and, even when he departs and returns to Japan, estranged from his own life.

On the surface, this is a familiar story: the traveller outside his element – and it's almost always a man – experiences something beyond what he ever imagined was sexually possible, after which he is changed, possessed, shattered. Think of the couple in Ian McEwan's *The Comfort of Strangers*, or, further back, any number of Celine's novels. Hirano chases far more delicate quarry here. Following his narrator into this maze of desire, we watch as a man tries to place a traumatic experience in a protective silo from his everyday life – only to realise he has walled himself inside the silo with it.

John Freeman

I

THEY WERE CROUCHING, naked, in a high-ceilinged room painted black.

Six men and six women, twelve people in all. Okada and Misa were the only Japanese.

The others were of various colours – seemingly by design – their straining, naked bodies illuminated by an enormous chandelier suspended like an explosion of silver and crystal.

Appearing to be in their twenties to their forties, they were tourists, like Okada and Misa, who had been deceived into coming, or perhaps abducted. None was Hungarian.

They found themselves in a seven-storey structure built in the late nineteenth century, in Pest. The entire structure seemed to belong to one person. The extravagant salon, with walls a rich crimson, was furnished with sofas, chests, and accessories in a contemporary, Neo-Baroque style of mainly black and silver.

First, there had been a dinner reception, where Okada and Misa spent a relaxing hour. Then, they were led up to the seventh floor, where they were held down, forcibly undressed, and locked in an inner room.

The black of the walls in this room was as lustrous as soft leather. There was a large white-rimmed mirror, also in the Neo-Baroque style. The windows were covered by thick curtains embroidered with gold arabesques, which a couple of the people had flung open, hoping for a way to escape, only to find the windows fitted with iron lattices.

Outside, an intense darkness had stretched out across the city, and only the lights along the Chain Bridge hinted at the presence of the Danube River below it.

The captives huddled in a marble alcove. A single, dark blue carpet filled the centre of the room, which nobody dared approach.

The women were trembling; some wrapped their arms around themselves, others hugged their knees. None of the men, Okada included, tried to cover their genitals any more.

Misa was next to him, hanging her head. He cast furtive glances in her direction, trying to see her face, but her long, straight hair blocked his view. Her pale, defenseless breasts were taut to the nipples. He imagined trying to grab them, fighting off other men's hands in order to do so, and winced as if he'd been stabbed.

The time for screaming and defiance had passed; silence reigned.

A young black man lay flat on the floor in front of the only exit. His left eye was swollen, looking like a crushed boiled egg. His nose was bloodied and broken, and the sweat on his chest glistened like pulverised diamonds; he was wheezing through his open mouth.

Okada pondered the man's firm musculature as if it were dressed meat in a display case. The image of him struggling, his long, thick penis swinging violently, was still branded in Okada's memory. The behemoths who had pummeled him into submission were standing guard outside the door.

Two men and two women, wearing masks, sat watching the captives. The men were dressed from the waist up, while everything below was exposed. The women wore black underwear and garter belts with bright red embroidery.

Yet another man, apparently the master of the house, sat in a Carver chair. Earlier he had greeted everyone cordially in the salon. Dressed in a paisley silk smoking jacket, his head shaved, he was the only observer without a mask. He was muscular, had deep-set eyes, and his skin, which seemed to have been scrubbed of any hint of a tan, had a meticulously tended glow.

He was gripping a black cane inlaid with stones, beaming a smile. His mouth, large enough to fit a fist, made him look more monstrous than any mask could. Occasionally he would murmur something to himself in Hungarian, which none of the captives could understand.

He had given the couples one and only one order: Right there, in front of everyone, to "make love".

~

Okada worked at a small trading company in Tokyo. He had come to Budapest alone to finalise an import agreement for propolis.

It was early November; unlike in Tokyo, where some days could bring lingering summer heat, in Budapest it was too cold to go out without a heavy coat.

That day he had finished his business earlier than expected and had the afternoon free. He was booked for a return flight the afternoon of the following day.

After going to see Heroes' Square, he walked down Andrássy Avenue, where he entered the Terror Háza, the House of Terror museum, which told of Hungary's dark history of fascism and communism. The Nazis had used the building during World War II; after the war, it was turned into the headquarters of the State Protection Authority, communist Hungary's secret police. Countless photos of victims were arrayed on a large wall, and in the basement there were re-creations of the cells where dissidents had been tortured. Okada had come in out of idle curiosity and had left, unsurprisingly, in a solemn mood. He went to the beguilingly beautiful former Postal Savings Bank, an art nouveau building designed by Ödön Lechner, which had been recommended by one of his Hungarian business partners, and took photos.

He walked to the Danube, where he admired the autumn foliage. He crossed the Chain Bridge, then took a cable car up Buda Castle Hill. He gazed out over the city for a long time, losing himself in the view. Bathed in the soft afternoon light, the city center below had a hazy allure. In something of a rapture, Okada promised himself to come back someday, when he had more time.

He followed the flow of people to the underground labyrinth of the castle. Within this multilayered network of natural caves was a bizarre tourist show made up of things like a fountain of wine and the head of a buried statue sticking out from the ground. His thoughts grew disjointed and he lost his way a few times, but he wasn't struck by anything in particular beyond the dim light and the mouldy smell. Before he knew it, he was outside.

He returned to Budapest and strolled around aimlessly, as if the city were a continuation of the labyrinth.

Hungarian doesn't belong to the Indo-European language family; it was apparently part of the Finno-Ugric branch of the Uralic family. This fact, which he had skimmed over in a guidebook, was brought home to him now. Although written in the Latin alphabet, the words on shop and road signs were completely unintelligible to him. The only one he could readily understand was on an advertisement for a porn shop: "Sex".

On impulse, he bought a silver cutlery set in an antique store.

Fatigue suddenly overcame him, and he decided to stop in a café to rest and consult his map before returning to the hotel, but this only made setting out again all the more difficult. He had a hot buttered rum to warm up, then called a server over to order a glass of red wine.

It was only then that he noticed a group of four people at the next table; one appeared to be Japanese. Her back was turned to him, but he caught a glimpse of her profile. She was wearing a dark gray cardigan, the sleeves rolled up, over a white shirt. Her collar was open; she was wearing a thin, pink-gold necklace, and a silver watch. Tight jeans, brown leather belt. She had long eyelashes, and the bridge of her nose was high and broad, giving her a vaguely sensual air. This was Misa.

She seemed to have noticed him first. The sun had started to set; he could see her reflection in the window, looking at him. Their eyes met that way.

"Are you . . . Japanese?" she asked in Japanese, turning back to him. The flirtatious way she tilted her head, the probing look in her eyes, the flicker of a smile between the words "you" and "Japanese", all led Okada to guess that these were words she had said many times before.

"Yes. I'm here on business. From Tokyo. And you, are you sightseeing?"

"I'm staying with the girl sitting across from me. She's Italian. And rich."

Her full, glossy lips parted, revealing bright, white teeth. She'd nodded toward a girl in a black knit cap, sitting at her table, who looked like a university student. The girl's thick eyebrows gave the impression of wilfulness, even as her small brown eyes seemed startled at Misa's glance in her direction. Her features were grown-up, but she was obviously quite young. She pursed her lips, as if feeling put upon, and turned away.

Misa turned back around and whispered something in the

girl's ear. He would learn later that her name was Federica. Misa was smiling, but Federica glared sternly and shook her head. Misa ignored her and moved to Okada's table.

"Is everything all right?" he asked.

"She's a lesbian."

"Oh."

"I'm not, but since she's letting me stay with her . . ."

"Since she's letting you stay with her . . . ?"

Federica didn't look angry so much as in pain.

It wasn't clear whether Misa was letting Federica have her body or not, but even if she were, it probably didn't happen regularly.

Thus Federica was psychologically a slave, enduring a situation that drove her to act out destructively against both Misa and herself. That, at least, was Okada's take as he looked at the pitiful resignation on her face.

Misa was twenty-eight, eight years younger than Okada. She said she had worked as a web designer for an IT firm in Tokyo, but about a year after the earthquake and tsunami of 2011 she took a trip to Paris, and had been traveling around Europe ever since. Judging from her purse and clothes, she wasn't exactly roughing it as a backpacker.

What originally beckoned her to Paris from Tokyo was a male acquaintance, whom she described to Okada as a novelist. She stayed with him for only a week, however, moving on to another friend in Brussels, then further north to Stockholm and south to Toledo, staying only a week or two in each. Several of her stops were places where there was nothing to see, where you couldn't even be sure which country you were in.

She met Federica in Rome over the summer. They went on a trip to Marrakesh, parted ways for a time, and then got back together. They had recently been in Zagreb and Bucharest. Since she could only remain "for a maximum of three months during the six months following the date of first entry" in the

European Union's Schengen Area, she had left for a time and had only returned a few days ago.

Okada counted on his fingers and asked, half-jokingly, "So you've been living the wandering life for more than half a year now?"

"At first I thought it would only be two weeks. I came on paid leave, then somehow wound up staying. I quit my job via email."

"Can one just quit like that? There are procedures, forms –"

"I can."

He paused. "I see. And you've been traveling alone the whole time?"

"Alone?" Misa smiled wryly. She looked at him as if she found him cute and naïve. "I've been with Federica ever since we met in Rome."

"Ah, right."

"We've had our ups and downs. She has severe mood swings and we argue a lot. But she's a really good person at heart."

"What made you want to stay abroad in the first place?"

"Have you ever lived abroad, Mr. Okada?"

"No, never."

"One shouldn't ask the Japanese living here such a question so lightly. Isn't it obvious that we have our reasons?"

Okada was taken aback. "Yeah, I guess so. I'm sorry."

Misa gave him a weary smile, and he shut his mouth. His shoes half off, he shifted his feet, which were tired and sore from hours of walking on cobblestone streets. Misa had accumulated six months' worth of that kind of fatigue all across Europe.

He couldn't guess what she was feeling. But having spent the year in Tokyo after the earthquake as she had, he imagined himself able to empathise, able somehow to understand her mental state.

"How much longer can you stay?"

Misa crossed her arms and planted her elbows on the table. She brushed the hair from her face. "I have to exit in two or three months . . . but I'll probably run out of money before then."

"Do you actually, really, know where you are right now?"

"Huh?"

"The latitude and longitude, this exact moment, right now."

Misa looked out the window. It was completely dark outside. Then she burst out laughing. "Mr. Okada, are you okay?" she asked, tilting her head. But Okada didn't laugh back. She seemed confused, but then realised what he was suggesting, and grew serious. She stared back at him. "Will you take me?" she asked. "Back to Japan?"

They had only just met, but Okada was enchanted and felt an irresistible attraction. "I'm returning tomorrow, changing planes in Helsinki. If you want, we can go back on the same flight."

Misa looked at him blankly, then lowered her head in thought. Without looking up, without a word, she nodded slightly.

She stayed with Okada, ignoring Federica entirely until the café began preparing for its dinner service. It was cruel, but Federica put up with it.

Misa checked the time and told Okada she wanted to have dinner with him somewhere. As they gathered their things, Federica approached them and introduced herself to Okada. She said, in English, that there was a party at a friend's house, and that she would like Misa and him to join her. Okada eyed Misa to gauge her intent: she shook her head.

Federica let out a scream and began to sob. The other customers in the café turned and stared. Without seeming at all surprised, Misa hugged her and began calming her down, as if this kind of thing happened all the time. She looked at Okada and asked him to come along if he didn't have other plans.

He agreed. He didn't want to leave Misa with Federica.

While they waited for the car that Federica had called,

Misa went to the restroom. The two others at their table were leaving, and Okada felt that Federica was giving him a meaningful glance. That is, although she had invited him to join them, she really wanted him just to go away. But then she smiled gently and asked him what was in his bag. Her eyes were still red from crying.

"Cutlery. Knives and forks and things."

She took a quick look inside.

"Like a knife cutting meat, your face only cuts off one piece and shows it."

Okada frowned. He wasn't confident in his comprehension of spoken English and hesitated to reply. Federica twisted her mouth and said the same thing again, slowly. He imagined a silver knife glinting in one of his eyes. He was about to ask her what she was trying to say, but she cut him off: "You can't understand Misa's true feelings. I can." She looked into his eyes to confirm that he had understood her.

Misa returned from the restroom. She too took an interest in the cutlery, which became the topic of conversation until a black Mercedes-Benz limousine pulled up.

The three of them got in. Okada was too distracted by the two women to pay attention to where they were going, or by what route. How was he supposed to interpret Federica's words? Misa claimed not to be lesbian. Was that true, or just something that she said to men? Or did she mean that she could swing both ways? Was Federica, out of jealousy, trying to warp his image of Misa? As he was turning over these questions, they arrived at the seven-storey building in Pest.

The party had already begun. Around thirty people in formal attire were standing around, eating and drinking. Okada felt out of place in his simple business suit, but the master of the house, the well-built man with a shaved head, raised his index finger and told him that dress didn't matter: what mattered was enjoying the occasion.

Federica gave the man a warm embrace; they chatted for a time, but then she was nowhere to be found. Okada and Misa wondered where she had gone and discussed the possibility of leaving. That's when they were led up to the seventh floor. The captives were released before dawn.

~

Okada and Misa got into the same limousine that had brought them to the party, and were let out in front of the Hungarian National Museum. It was still dark and the streets were empty.

"You sure you want to get out here?" the driver asked dubiously. Okada didn't want him to know where he was staying. From there it was about a ten-minute walk to the hotel. He expected Misa to stay in the car and be taken to Federica's place, but she took his arm and said, "I'm coming too."

Before leaving, the driver looked back again and said, "Don't tell anybody about what happened tonight. Got it? This isn't coming from the boss, this is just my advice to you. Forget all about it, the sooner the better. All right?"

Okada just looked at him without nodding. The car drove off.

He felt like a laughing-stock, standing there on the empty street, holding the bag of silver cutlery that he'd been careful not to forget.

Back in his hotel room, they took turns showering. Misa wanted to take her time, so she let Okada go first. As the hot water struck his thoroughly chilled body, he thought back on everything that had happened.

He hadn't yet been able to feel free of the night. Although they got out of the car blocks away from the hotel, any native of the city would be able to guess from the drop-off spot that this was where he was staying. He had been on the alert to any sign of trouble once back in the hotel, but all seemed normal. He felt relieved to be back in his room.

The captives hadn't "made love" all at once. Rather, the spectators had amused themselves with different "ensembles" of pairings and sex acts. A different piece of background music was played on request for each round. Okada remembered string quartets by Schulhoff and Ullmann, as well as Messiaen's *Quartet for the End of Time*. When a man in a tuxedo requested the scherzo from Shostakovich's String Quartet No. 11, though, the spectators burst out laughing and started arguing with each other in Hungarian.

The captives had been promised that, as long as they followed orders, they would be released by dawn, with one condition: if even a single person disobeyed, they would be held indefinitely.

The first couple to perform didn't put up any resistance, and perhaps that's why those who followed also obeyed. A kind of order emerged, woven out of intertwined threads of hope that the night would end soon and resignation that, if they wanted it to, they had no choice but to do as told. The black man who'd been beaten earlier was held down and raped by two white men, the marble floor streaked with blood from his violation. Okada shuddered at the sight, terrified that something similar awaited him. Some were called back into the thick of things time and again; Okada and Misa, for some reason, weren't summoned to mix in with the others.

Only after everyone else had been subjected to every kind of humiliation were they called upon to perform. Their orders came directly from the master of the house: They were to "make love", just the two of them, in "the Japanese style". The female spectators, who were sipping tea, smiled at this.

Okada hesitated. The others, who had already fulfilled their orders, made no effort to hide their irritation. To them, Okada and Misa looked as if they were already lovers; their assignment seemed hardly an ordeal. It would be a sweet spectacle, the evening's dessert. Their impatience reached a boil: "Hurry up!" they shouted, booing and jeering.

Misa took Okada's hand and led him to the dark blue carpet. She looked at the spectators and then kissed him. At the master's wordless signal, Ligeti's *Lux Aeterna* began to play. Was this the piece that brought these proceedings to a close?

Misa tried everything she could, but Okada was unresponsive. A woman in a red butterfly mask couldn't contain a fit of giggling, but the master of the house silenced her with a finger to the lips.

Okada felt miserable, lying on the carpet, unable to get an erection. In this domain, effort had no bearing on success. Misa smiled and gently stroked his chest and his cheeks to comfort him. He closed his eyes and tried to focus on her. He recalled his first glimpse of her in the café, and their promise to return to Japan together. Wasn't this something that they eventually would have done together anyway?

He got on top of her. He buried his face in her breasts and inhaled the smell of her skin. He could feel her warmth against the tip of his organ, and then, slowly, it was engulfed. They locked eyes and then closed them; when one's eyes opened the other's would too. Their lips touched. Misa licked the inside of his mouth gently. They made love, forgetting all about the order to do so in "the Japanese style".

When they were done, the room was quiet. No one said anything, no one laughed. A woman tore off her mask and began sobbing. The man who had been stroking himself beside her turned and tended to her.

Okada finished his shower and climbed into bed, still in his bathrobe. He stared absently at the white ceiling. There was no giant chandelier there, illuminating the room with its brilliant light. The bathroom was also silent, save for the water running. He could faintly make out the sound of crying.

Forty minutes later she came out, in a bathrobe, hair wet. They had now, individually and alone, washed away all traces of their intercourse.

Okada brewed two cups of coffee. Misa took hers to the window and opened the curtain. The window clouded over with the steam from her coffee, then cleared up. He saw that it was growing increasingly light outside, and was reminded of how much time had passed since the previous evening in the café.

Misa turned to look back at him, a troubled expression on her face. "I'm sorry," she said, as if that were the one thing she absolutely had to say.

Okada hadn't expected this. He hadn't thought for a second that she would apologise, even though it was clear he had been the pawn in the turmoil between the two women.

But it was also clear that in their so-called lovemaking, Misa hadn't performed just so that she could get out of there. He realised now, for the first time, that there was also an element of atonement: she had wanted to help him escape as well. Okada now wondered what it meant that, during those hours of captivity, he never once felt hatred toward her.

He reminded her: "The plane leaves at one. Let's go back together."

He went to her side and held her in his arms. She let the empty coffee cup fall to the floor and yielded to his embrace. She pressed her cheek against his chest in his half-open bathrobe. Soon, without either of them initiating it, they were naked. They kissed and held each other, even as cold from the window chilled them. She clung to him, as if she might collapse at any moment. He bent his knees and arched his back to support her weight. The water from her wet hair flowed into the crevices of their bodies. They needed this, to stay like this for a long time, soaking in the still-pure, newly born light of the sun.

Keiichirō Hirano

II

NOTHING CHANGED IN OKADA'S life after returning to Japan. He lived alone in his condominium and went to work in the mornings. He did his job, day after uneventful day, and returned home in the evenings. The shipments from the firm in Budapest arrived without problem. His colleagues at work had no inkling of the nightmare he had lived through during his trip. He, on the other hand, couldn't forget it. He simply couldn't believe that he was home, back where he had lived all his life. Again and again he relived the experiences in Budapest. One day, the memories flowing from one to another, he recalled his time in the underground labyrinth of Buda Castle, and was suddenly seized by a convulsion deep in his chest. When he was actually making his way through the labyrinth, he hadn't felt any particular agitation, but as he thought about it now, that was precisely why it was significant: he had, in the same way, without his knowing it, been wandering in a labyrinth, lost. It was a transparent labyrinth whose walls he couldn't see.

He didn't know when and where he might have entered it. Was it when he set foot, completely by chance, in the café where he met Misa? Or was it before that, while he was meandering through the city, heedless of the road signs along the way?

Or was it even earlier? In the months after the earthquake? Or even earlier than that? All he understood was that it was not until he was ordered to "make love" in that locked room that he first sensed being in the labyrinth, and that the room was a dead end.

He had no idea where in the labyrinth he was now. Its walls couldn't be seen, or touched, and the world outside wasn't obscured by even a trace of fog. How would he find the way out? He didn't know where to begin.

Had the walls been made out of clay or brick, anyone outside wouldn't know that somebody was lost inside. But ultimately, even with transparent walls, there was no way for them to notice who was trapped there.

He was forced to walk along those invisible walls. From time to time he would hit a dead end, turn around, and try to take a different path, only to find himself somehow once again following the same path as before.

There were moments when he felt, for one reason or another, that the walls were reflecting the winter sunlight, or that he could see smudges left by somebody's hand. Those glimmers were revelations of the labyrinth's reality, but when he reached out to touch them, they proved to be phantoms.

Misa never showed that afternoon at Ferenc Liszt Airport.

She'd returned to Federica's apartment to retrieve her passport. Okada had offered to go with her, but she shook her head. "I don't want to provoke her." She'd said it as an afterthought, but it seemed reasonable.

He waited for her at the airport. Right before check-in for the flight closed, he received an email from her: "I'm sorry. It's impossible for me to return to Japan today." He immediately rang her, but she didn't pick up. He worried she was being held against her will. He left a voicemail and sent an email saying he would rescue her if necessary. Her email reply came quickly: "I'm quite all right. I hope one day we can meet again." End of message. This made him even more suspicious; he rashly considered cancelling his flight and searching for her, despite having no idea where she might be.

He was in pieces; her change of heart was a betrayal. He felt freshly wounded, the pain throbbing, his heart racing, helpless. How could she do this to him? It was Misa, not Federica, that he found himself furious at. If she had written those emails under duress, she could have at least said something in Japanese, like "help", without Federica's knowing. No, this was Misa's decision, this was her betrayal.

He saw now how shallow their intimacy had been, how tarnished her early-morning apology in the hotel. He had been so moved when she said it. What a fool he was. He could hear Federica saying: "You can't understand Misa's true feelings." He hated that that was true.

Okada didn't try to contact Misa after returning to Japan. It wouldn't be true to say he didn't hope to hear from her, but no word came.

He felt as if his entire life had been made into a mockery. Not by her, but by the depravity of the world itself.

He felt powerless, but the feeling was fundamentally different from that of having expectations for the future, planning accordingly, and then suffering every possible setback. His life, the life he lived moment by moment, was now laughable. His past seemed drenched with stench and slime, as if he'd stepped barefoot onto rotten fruit.

Many times he thought how his nightmare, if told to friends, would make an amusing tale: Japanese man travels abroad and is forced by a shadowy, depraved foreign millionaire to have sex with a Japanese woman he's just met. People would be titillated, tantalised, by a story so outlandish, perhaps even made envious. Of course he wasn't going to tell anybody anything. The root of his suffering was not the acts that he had been forced to perform. It was the embraces and emotions he had exchanged with Misa after they had been released.

Only one thing could have avenged the humiliation that they'd endured that night, and that was for them to make love, truly, out of the spectators' sight. That was their only hope, the only way to demystify the ritualised lewdness that they had offered up to that degeneracy.

And isn't that precisely what had happened? In the sanctum of the fresh morning sun, hadn't they truly made love?

But all he felt for Misa now was hatred and contempt. He wished misfortune upon her, imagined her suffering worse wounds, deeper wounds, only to realise the futility of his response and rebound into self-hatred and the burning desire to see her again. Loneliness filled the core of his being. There was nobody other than Misa whom he could love with abandon, and whose love could console him. He realised that he loved her. And could do nothing about it.

The year turned. It was early February, when light snowflakes fluttered from the sky.

Okada was on a subway platform, heading home from work, when an email arrived from Misa. She had returned to Japan a week earlier and was, at that moment, in Hibiya. He tried to ignore the message, but that proved impossible. He called her, heard her voice, and made plans to see her immediately.

When he arrived in the hotel, she was sitting in the lobby, waiting for him. At first, she looked away, as if she didn't recognise him, only to do a double-take. For his part, Okada's memory of her face had also grown hazy – surprising, given all the time he had spent thinking about her.

"Long time no see," he said.

"Oh . . . yes, long time no see."

"You look a little thinner."

"Yes . . . that's what being back in Japan will do," she replied.

"So what happened? After I left."

"I kept wandering around Europe. After three months of that, I came back to Japan."

"What about Federica?" Okada asked.

"We broke up. For good."

"I see."

They had dinner in the hotel's dining room. Beginning with her real name, they awkwardly picked up their relationship where they had left it off.

It turned out that Misa was actually Misaki. Okada somehow hadn't expected this. She said that "Misa" was easier for foreigners to pronounce, that she had never liked her real name anyway, that she wanted him to keep calling her "Misa".

Gradually, she began to relax. She didn't seem embarrassed about everything that had happened, she smiled more than she had when they'd first met in Budapest, and she seemed to have lost the air of vagabondage that he had found so appealing.

He was surprised by the cheerful charm she radiated as they spoke. Why had she changed? Was it because she and Federica had broken up? And yet, if this had been the Misa in that café in Budapest, he probably wouldn't have accepted Federica's invitation to go to the party, nor would Federica have suffered as she had. He would have exchanged two, maybe three words with the Japanese woman who had started a conversation with him. At most he would have amiably chatted with her, and then gone back to his hotel to eat dinner alone. Nothing would have happened. Nothing in his daily life would have changed. He wouldn't have gone through hell.

Still, the woman before him was unquestionably Misa. He looked at her intently. She'd been drinking red wine. She looked back at him, somewhat puzzled, then smiled, her teeth gleaming between her full lips.

This, all of this, was now their reality after everything that had happened in Budapest. Whether she was now as melancholy as she had been before, or had been as cheerful then as she was now, it wouldn't change the fact that she had been mocked and taunted right alongside him, that she had endured as much as he had.

He felt the need to explain himself. After they finished eating, after a bit of silence, he finally spoke: "During these three months, I really started to hate you. I just couldn't forgive you for how you left me. I wanted you to get hurt. Or, probably, worse."

Misa's eyes widened, but she just nodded without saying anything.

Okada didn't dare to ask why she hadn't come to the airport. Instead, he said: "Even then, I wanted to see you again."

Misa looked down silently. Then, she suddenly laughed, exactly as she had in the café.

They spent the night together. Time folded; the future reconnected to the past.

At many points throughout the night, lost in ecstasy under the dim light, Okada perceived in Misa's face the shadow of the masks worn by the spectators in Budapest. He didn't try to think what that might mean.

~

The happiness Okada felt at resuming his relationship with Misa was so ordinary that it felt almost anticlimactic.

He discovered things about her that he admired and loved, things that may have been flattened out of view by the unique situation they had first found themselves in.

A Cameroonian, who must have been six-and-a-half feet tall,

lived on the same floor as Okada. Late one night, drunk and naked, he staggered out of his apartment and started pushing all the buzzers in the vestibule. The other residents were too frightened to leave their apartments, but Misa, who sometimes stayed over, went up to him with a smile, turned him around, and led him back to his apartment.

It was a small thing, to be sure, yet Okada was deeply impressed by her character, kindness, and fearlessness. Was it because of who she was that she'd been able to travel through Europe for nine months? Or was it her travels through Europe that made her who she was now? It didn't matter, really, but as far into the past as the night in Budapest might recede, this Misa resonated with the image of her on top of him, in front of the spectators, heroically doing everything she could in the face of his impotence.

He confessed to her that, even now, he couldn't shake the feeling of being surrounded by spectators, of people watching, in intimate moments.

"I think maybe the worst part for you is imagining it. You don't know what we looked like," she said. Then after a bit, she added, "What if we tried making a video so we can see for ourselves?"

"A video? Of us having sex?"

"Yes. Memories don't stay the same. They say that every time you remember something, you write over a memory. If you remember that night tonight, tomorrow you won't be able to remember it in any other way than you did tonight. If we shoot a video and watch it together, then the memory of that night will be written over. Instead of trying to erase the memory, we could paint over it with the memory of us now."

Okada was astonished. He would never have thought of anything like this. In theory, as weird as it was, it offered hope for relief from the image in his mind. And, although it was something he had never tried, he knew that many couples enjoyed such things now.

He set up the video camera to shoot from the side of the bed, leaving the room lights on.

He pushed the record button. They said nothing, signaling each other with their eyes, smiling to ease the tension. They undressed and embraced as they had many times before. Each wave of pleasure made them feel less inhibited, and they allowed themselves the freedom to make love as they wished.

There was a fresh excitement in having every move recorded, with no distinctions between the beautiful and the ugly, the tender and the comical. He could see how some got addicted to this.

The action they'd videotaped played on the large 42-inch screen. They were naked as they watched, bundled in the duvet. Okada had seen himself on video, in normal circumstances, only a few times, but he had certainly never seen his own naked butt like this before. It was completely different from inspecting a boil or a pimple in the mirror. Here he was closely observing the contractions and relaxations of the muscles, the interactions of over a hundred pounds of mass that didn't stay still for a moment.

He remembered being conscious of the lens, and caught himself on screen looking into the camera a few times. He saw in his face an expression he had never known before. Do I always look like that? he thought. He clearly looked satisfied. His pleasure and Misa's meshed nicely, like gears; but more than that, he was so obviously satisfied at knowing that he was the one turning those gears that it was almost comical. He was stunned by his simple lust for conquest, and had to smile at the sight of himself brimming with rapturous complacency. And yet, as he'd suspected, this exercise was all merely a brief diversion.

It didn't validate their relationship in any fundamental way; it tickled it, bent it, convulsed it, tweaked it, and nothing more.

Okada felt, though, that Misa's hunch had been right. When he was making love he was conscious only of being recorded, and forgot all about the spectators' gaze. Indeed, now it was the two of them who were watching.

They tried different experiments in recording themselves, and watched the results together afterwards. The sudden ebbing of male desire that follows ejaculation led Okada to watch somewhat abstractedly, in a quiet frame of mind.

The nightmare lodged in his memory was written over again and again, it changed form, and, in time it grew dim. When he tried to remember it, the image that came was of the two of them frolicking playfully in front of the spectators. No longer was he impotent. She was smiling. They were the captives, but also the captors. They took orders, but also gave them. They were the performers, but also the spectators.

"What . . . what actually happened?"

"What do you mean?"

One evening after watching a video Okada slowly, deliberately, posed the question to Misa. "That night. Federica told them what she wanted us to do, right? She was in love with you. She wanted revenge. Isn't that why she had them do that to us?"

"Maybe not everybody who was brought to that party was a victim," she said.

"You mean they were complicit? Part of the scene? Decoys? After that first couple set the tone by following orders, everyone else just kind of went along. Maybe their submissiveness was a performance, planned in advance. Maybe the others, too . . . Maybe they enjoyed it as a kind of live pornography. Maybe only the ones who were beaten and bloodied were real victims . . ."

"Does it matter anymore?" Misa cut in. "I had almost forgotten about it."

Okada decided not to press the issue. "I'm sorry," he said. "I've started forgetting about it too. That's precisely why I'm thinking about it so much. But I won't bring it up again."

He got dressed and started preparing dinner. Misa came in to help, and pulled a cutlery set out of the sideboard. "What are these?" she asked. "They're beautiful. Are they antiques? They're a little tarnished, though."

He looked at the cutlery, then at her, puzzled. "Those are the ones I bought that day. I just put them away and never used them."

"That day?"

"Yeah . . . I guess you don't remember. No matter."

He cocked his head a bit and took the set from her hands. On the spot he decided to get rid of it – he didn't want any reminders of the day – and slipped the set into an old shopping bag to be tossed into the garbage.

~

Not long after that, Misa broke off contact again.

Okada was alone once more. The difference this time was that he tried repeatedly to contact her. She didn't answer his calls or return his emails. Because their meetings had always been at his place, he didn't even know where she lived.

What had happened? He thought over the half year they had spent together. He replayed the events of the last month. He re-watched the images they had recorded, searching her face for a hint of something.

But he came up empty. She was gone, and the fact that all he had left of her were those videos made his loneliness even worse. Once again he was tormented by the spectators' gaze, even though Misa was no longer there.

He'd been wandering in the transparent labyrinth all

along, after all. He found himself thrown back to that night
in Budapest.

Two months passed. Suddenly, it seemed, chill was in the air, and
Okada wore a trench coat to work for the first time that season.
The summer had carelessly allowed itself to drag out, and when
autumn finally appeared it had the anxious face of one who
wouldn't be staying long.

After Okada got home from work one evening, out of the blue
he received an email from Misa. She asked if she could come pay
him a visit. He stared at the computer and thought, and kept
thinking as he changed out of his work clothes. He finally wrote
back that he wouldn't mind. Thirty minutes later, his doorbell
rang.

He opened the door, and there, in front of his eyes, one
woman became two.

He thought he was hallucinating; he shook his head, closed
his eyes, opened them, closed them again, and then he began to
understand.

~

"Misa" were twin sisters. Misato he had met in Budapest. Misaki
he had been involved with for half a year.

They sat opposite from him at the dining table.

He seemed to be looking not at twins, but at the two paths
that his life had taken, if uncertainly: the life in which he and
Misa – the Misa with whom he spent that terrifying night in
Budapest – were reunited in Japan, and the life in which they
weren't, having been replaced by Misaki. Rather than two
people, they were like two different worlds coexisting in front
of him. He even began to entertain the illusion that he was two
people, each of whom had lived in those different worlds.

The sisters looked identical, yet they were two; but in Okada's mind the Misa he had known recently had overwritten the Misa he had known in Budapest. The body he had embraced on that dark blue carpet on the marble floor was now just a trace, one that had been replaced by the body he had made love with countless times on his own bed. But something about the memory of Misato seemed to be seeping into his image of Misaki, as if she were somehow trying to resist being erased.

Entirely perplexed, Okada asked for an explanation.

Misaki, who was the younger of the two, was the one to respond:

Misato couldn't just go back to Japan without saying good-bye to Federica. Federica apologised tearfully for what she had done, Misato wound up forgiving her, stayed with her, and gave up any hope of having a future with Okada.

For one thing, she didn't think that she could get over those terrible memories. As long as she was with Okada, there was no way she could ever forget. She decided never to contact him again, but he still weighed on her mind. When she did return to Japan, she told Misaki what had happened and convinced her to meet Okada in her place. They had impersonated each other several times before. Even if Misaki didn't explicitly end the relationship, leaving it ambiguous would allow things to fade.

But as it turned out, she liked Okada at first sight, exactly as Misato had. She understood for herself why her sister liked him. She began to wonder what Misato's real intentions were.

Regardless of what her sister wanted, Misaki originally planned to tell Okada honestly that she was Misato's twin sister. It would have been difficult, however, to get him to believe her and not think that it was some kind of a prank. As she vacillated over what to do, it became clear that Okada believed that she was her sister, without a trace of doubt. And then, when he said that he had "hated" Misato, those words struck a chord. Didn't she hate her sister as well? Truly hated her, even while loving her.

Unlike Misato, she had no bad memories with Okada. She knew that those bad memories were precisely what kept him obsessed with her, but still, what if she just let that be?

In the beginning she didn't think about it too deeply. Slowly, though, their love became something that she couldn't give up. She began to ask herself whether somebody could really love another on the basis of a single event. Could a single shared experience be the thing that gave birth to love? Wasn't it, rather, that one loved everything about the other person? The truth was that Okada loved her, Misaki. After everything that had happened between them since the night in Budapest, he loved her more than her sister. That was more or less what she told him, all related in the cerebral manner that Okada knew so well.

Misato stayed silent and expressionless throughout. Only once, when Misaki was talking about the love-hate relationship that she had with her, did she look down, disconsolate, and shake her head slightly.

Okada could understand, intellectually, how he and Misaki came to get involved and how their relationship had deepened, but emotionally, it was difficult to accept.

"When were you planning on telling me the truth? Did you think I would just go along with it?"

"I've been thinking about doing it these past two months. But what do you mean, 'go along with it'?"

"I was in love with your sister, not you. You may be twins, but you're different people, aren't you? You two should know that even better than I do."

"How can you say such a thing?"

"What do you mean?"

"The way you two met was what it was, of course," Misaki

said. "But we were together for six months. When I left, who did you miss? Wasn't it me, not her? Wasn't it the memories you made with me that you looked back on?"

"You . . . you're attractive, there's no question about that. But after getting dragged into that crazy business with Misato, I was somehow able to bounce back, and I was just trying to live my life when you came along. Of course, after everything that had happened, seeing you . . . It got to me. When you talk about how Misato and I met, it wasn't like our eyes met in a train station. You'll never understand what we went through."

"So? Does that mean you can't love me? That you don't love me?"

Okada wanted to object, but the more he tried to put his feelings into words, the further those words seemed to drift from what he was really feeling.

He looked back on the last six months. Even if their relationship hadn't started on false pretenses, wouldn't he still love her well enough? Misaki, that is, not Misato.

"Misato can't love you. She doesn't love you. But I do."

Before Misato could open her mouth, Misaki had cut in. The competition between the two sisters was something that Okada couldn't fathom. But the cunning of Misaki, who had invested enough time to be sure that there was no going back for him before she confessed the truth, seemed greatly to resemble the wanderlust of her sister, who spent nine months travelling around Europe relying on the kindness of others and driving Federica to despair.

Misato shrugged and sighed. Then she looked at Okada, a flicker of a smile in her eyes. That look, it took him back to that café in Budapest at nightfall. That look of ennui, somehow unique to her, drew him in, and he felt heartsick. What exactly was it that he loved about "Misa"? The more he thought about it, the harder it became to tell the difference between these two human beings who had been blended together in his imagination.

"What do you think?" he asked Misato, as if cross-examining her. "You're also an interested party here. Is it how she – is it how Misaki says it is?"

"Pretty much. If you're in love with me, isn't my sister close enough? Do you have to make things difficult?"

"Is that really how you feel?"

"We're genetically identical. We grew up in the same house, the same environment. They say only our immune systems are different. But that's not what's bothering you, is it?"

"I'm trying to be serious here."

"Mr. Okada, if you got involved with me, you would only regret it. We might look the same, but my sister is smarter than I am, and more stable. She can be trusted not to go running off to wander the globe. If you wonder how things might have been if we'd met again in Japan, it's easy: I would have never forgotten what happened that night. And neither would you. We would have been miserable, and broken up a long time ago."

Now more than ever Okada keenly felt himself being watched. Again and again they command: "Make love!" He hesitates, while the people who already had been forced to have sex angrily goad him on.

"What do you plan to do now?" he asked Misato.

"I don't know. I don't really want to stay in Japan . . . I might go back to Federica."

"Federica?" Okada frowned.

Misato allowed a hesitant, melancholy smile. He couldn't tell if she'd meant it what she said, or it was a bad joke. But the mere fact that she was willing to say Federica's name probably meant that she honestly wanted nothing more to do with him.

He finally understood why she had so captivated him: he had met her in the labyrinth. She was the only other human

being there. That day, in that blind alley, they were alone
together. Yet now, no matter how close he wanted to feel to
her, he knew there was a wall separating them. That morning
in Budapest, over the course of just a few hours, they had gone
their separate ways.

He was quiet for a long time.

~

Three days later, Misaki came again to visit, alone. Okada
had just eaten dinner and was sitting on the sofa, mulling the
situation over. He hadn't sorted his feelings out about her, but
meeting her like this, without Misato along, made it feel as if the
matter had already been decided.

He poured a cup of coffee and brought it to her. It was
a trivial gesture, but she took the cup with almost maudlin
emotion.

After a while she looked up and said, "Could you . . . could you
show me the videos we made together?"

"The videos? Now?"

"Yes. From the beginning."

He really wasn't in the mood to watch them, but they were
just videos, after all, and he did not say no.

As requested, he began the playback. Perhaps this was
meant to be one last viewing before he deleted them. It was
about time to do that, anyway.

Misaki sat on the bed close to him, and watched their
awkward fumbling at the beginning of the first video with bated
breath. The lights had been turned down, and the glow from the
screen deepened the shadows in her face. The volume was set
low, but their wordless voices seemed to steal into every last
corner in the room.

Okada stared at the two entwined naked bodies, bodies he

had seen many times before. Suddenly he caught a scent beside him, near the back of his neck, and a jolt went through him. He looked at her, startled, speechless. She must have felt his gaze, but refused to look back at him.

Why had he assumed that she was Misaki?

They grew less inhibited, and after the third video she asked, "Aren't we going to make one today?" He looked into her eyes. They sparkled just as they had when she looked up at him, kneeling on the marble floor, the crystal of the chandelier reflected in her eyes.

Before the fourth video could begin, he stopped the playback and set up the video camera. He pressed the record button and they began taking off each other's clothes.

They were playful, tickling and tantalising. They clung to each other, locked lips, sank into breathless ecstasy. They expressed their love not only for each other, but for the future that they should have shared.

He let the camera keep running even after they were done. They lay naked on the bed without saying a word.

Misa eventually got up. "I should go," she murmured.

"You're leaving?"

She paused. "Yes. Could you make a copy of tonight's video for me?"

"Yeah. Sure."

"I'll hold on to it for a while. I'll erase it at some point. But for now, I want it."

As he saw her out the door, they embraced and kissed once more. The memory of that evening in Budapest had already been written over many times. But the memory of that dawn by the hotel window had never been overwritten, had been preserved, just as it was. And yet, by tomorrow, that memory would have blended with this moment right now, would probably be recalled in a new way altogether.

The automatic lights went out, detected the motion of their bodies, and came back on.

This moment, their moment, would not swell into an eternity. But eternity grows bored and sometimes, whimsically, disguises itself as ordinary moments like this.

Okada saw Misato off.

She receded into the distance. Now it was probably only a matter of time before he met Misaki again, somewhere in a corner of the labyrinth.

About the Project

Keshiki is a series of chapbooks showcasing the work of some of the most exciting writers working in Japan today, published by Strangers Press, part of the UEA Publishing Project.

Each story is beautifully translated and presented as an individual chapbook, with a design inspired by the text.

Keshiki is a unique collaboration between University of East Anglia, Norwich University of the Arts, and Writers' Centre Norwich, funded by the Nippon Foundation.

Supported by